Bullfrog is the Best

Written by Alison Hawes

Illustrated by Gabriele Antonini

One fine June day, Bullfrog pulled himself on to the bank by the pond.

The sun was bright and he could see himself in the water.

"I am big and strong," he thought.

"I am the best!"

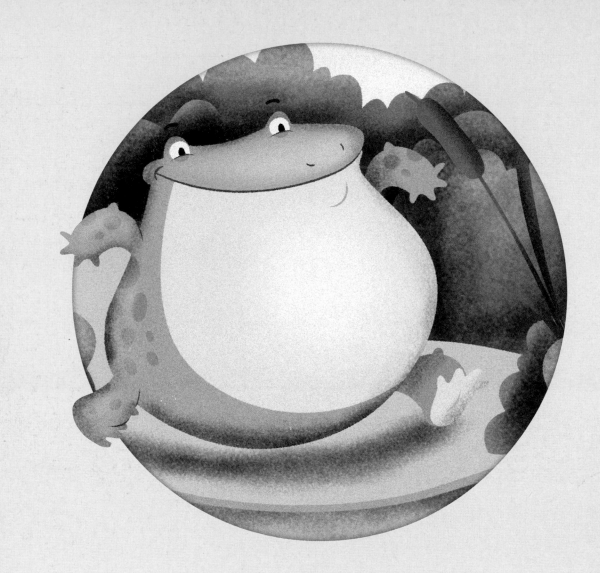

Then Bullfrog pushed his way through
the bulrushes to see who he could tell.

Soon he came across some newts.

"I am the biggest and the best,"
boasted Bullfrog.
"Yes, it is true!" agreed the newts.

Next Bullfrog met a bull standing
under a yew tree.
"I am bigger and better than you,"
he told the bull.

"You are big," mooed the bull,
chewing on a bush. "But the truth is,
bulls are much bigger than bullfrogs."

"I do not wish to seem rude," said
Bullfrog, "but that just CAN NOT
be true!"

Bullfrog yelled to the newts.
"Come and meet this bull," he said.

"Now, who is bigger, the bull or me?"
Bullfrog asked the newts.
"The bull!" they all cried.

Bullfrog stood up and pushed out his chest. He puffed and blew until he was full of air.

"Tell me the truth. Who looks bigger?" asked Bullfrog.
"The bull is still bigger!" said the newts.

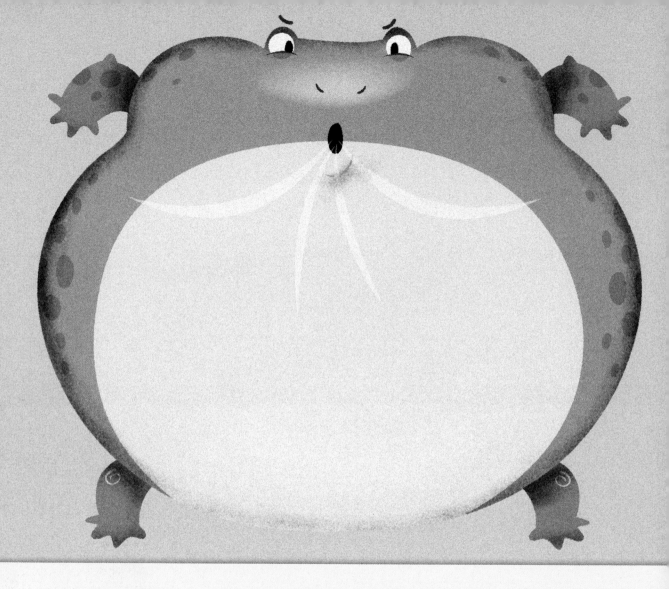

So Bullfrog puffed and blew again.
And as he blew, he grew and GREW!

"Stop that!" pleaded the newts.
"You could get hurt!" bellowed the bull.
But Bullfrog refused to stop.

In fact, Bullfrog was so full of air,
he flew up in the big, bright, blue sky
and was never seen again!